EMAILS
TO
A PARANORMAL

THE DIARY POEMS OF

Damien Darrk

V.T. Dacquino

2014

A VTD EduCon Book

Published by
VTD EduCon Books
Mahopac, NY 10541

For further information go to:
www.vtdacquino.com

ISBN:0-9904814-0-9
EAN-13:978-0-9904814-0-9

Emails to a Paranormal is a work of fiction and not intended to portray any real persons or events

To:

June, Jamie, Vinny,

Christian and Cadence

Special thanks to Jeff Edrich and Steve Haggerty for their help with formatting the manuscript and to the Mahopac Library Writers Group for helping to keep literacy alive in Mahopac --and in me.

Table of Contents

CHAPTER I

My Name

Part 1

I

I know you may find my name

To be strange

And may think that no caring parent

Would name a child

Damien Darrk

The truth is

I've created this name to protect my identity

And will tell you my real name

Only when I know

You can be trusted

II

I am being visited

By a spirit

I suspect she is a young girl

On a mission

The reason she has chosen my room

And me

A seventeen year old boy

May be connected to why

My father was killed

And why I am coming to you

III

She'll come again tonight

After midnight

When the house is quiet

Whispering behind my closet door

And moaning too

As she's done for months

I'm not afraid

And know I must help her

But I am helpless

Without you

IV

I've chosen you

To receive these diary poems

Because of your ability to communicate

With spirits

And I believe

As you do

That there are no coincidences

When it comes to matters of the supernatural

I also believe as you do

That dead people live here

V

She came to me

Several months ago

On Oct 30

The night of my birthday

My mother threw a surprise party

And when it was over

I went to my room

Where something called to me

From my closet

Moaning

VI

I wasn't sure what I was hearing

I laughed to myself

Thinking I was being pranked

"Come out," I said

"I know you geeks are in there"

But no one answered

And the moaning continued

I pulled the covers off

And walked to the door at the foot of my bed

The moaning got louder

VII

I felt coldness

Coming from the closet

But not like any coldness I've ever felt

It seeped through my skin

And entered me from every pore

I reached for the doorknob

Wishing to end the silly prank

But the knob was already turning

And the door opened

To an almost empty room

VIII

My clothes hung from hangers

Like ghosts

Unmoving

The shelf above them motionless

And from somewhere on the floor

In the corner of the darkness

The moaning

Became a whimper

Like a puppy without a mother

Crying for help

IX

I dropped to my knees
And listened as the whining
Took on a strange rhythm
Song like
Childlike
A lullaby that mothers use
To quiet their children
And then there was silence
Until I heard
My own mother's voice behind me

X

I gave her a poor excuse
For kneeling by my closet
At midnight
And have given her a dozen more excuses
For my strange behaviors
She doesn't understand any of this
And so I'm turning to you
To shed some light
On the mystery that is haunting my room
And me

Part 2

I

Somehow

I managed to sleep the night of my birthday

And spent most of the next day, Halloween

At my computer web-searching your name

Halloween is not my favorite holiday

My father died last year

On Halloween night

Returning from a three day business trip

Rushing to get home

To my mother and me

II

When the police arrived

To tell us about the accident

We thought they were trick-or-treaters

Until we answered the door and saw their faces

I stood there

By my mother

With candy to give them

But they were only there

To give us

Their condolences

III

My father

Was a very good father

He gave me everything

I needed

And even what I didn't

My memories of him

Will live with me forever

And I am grateful for the time we spent together

But I need your help

To contact him

IV

My mother

Is lonely

She wanders around our house

Like he will suddenly appear as he was

To hold her

As he used to

But we both know

That good husbands

And good fathers

Don't live in this world forever

V

I imagine

That you

In your line of work as a paranormal

Have communicated with ghosts

Like my father

Or the girl in my closet

Who may have been taken suddenly

Without a chance

To say

Good-bye

VI

Do you see them

And hear them

Out there

Floating in some weird haze

Moaning in closets

Or hovering frantically

Over the cars they've been killed in

Still trying to drive home

To families

They'll never reach

VII

How closely do I have to listen
To hear their whispers in the wind
Or separate the ticking of the clock
From the tapping of their fingers
On my brain
Or recognize that I must be dreaming
When the girl from the closet
Floats close enough
To brush my cheeks
With hers

VIII

Have you ever lost people you loved
Do you feel them
When you lie awake in the night
Do they talk to you in words
Or come in cold rushes through you
And do they pull across your skin
Like a ballerina's tights
Hugging closely to you
Making it impossible
For you to breathe

IX

Do dead people die
Or do they linger here
In some kind of temporary prison
Can I see them if I try
Can they see me
How dead Is dead
I know who you are
I've seen you on the computer
Do you say what you believe
And believe the things you say

X

These poems should have arrived to you by now
Please read them
I need you to come to her
Does she speak for herself
Or my father
Can you tell me what she wants from me
Please don't be afraid
I am different from most kids my age but not insane
If you believe in what you say
Then please believe in me

Part 3

I

I haven't heard back from you
But I know how busy you are
I check your web site
To follow your activities
You'll be speaking tonight
About the ghosts in your book
At a local coffee house
Please make time to write to me
She knows
That I have contacted you

II

Her whining was deafening
But it has quieted some
And she ventures out more often
Hovering
Around my room
Avoiding contact
Clinging desperately to the walls
Like a blown up balloon
Rubbed against a kid's hair
Charged with static electricity

III

She came at first

As a face without an expression

Floating

Above me

And I awoke in my bed

Sweating and startled

But not afraid of her

I knew somehow

She wasn't there

To harm me

IV

She has now learned

How to enter my dreams

I see her

As she must have looked

Before her death

Pretty

With long blonde hair

Hanging to her shoulders

And blue

Piercing eyes

V

I see her

In my sleep

Running alone

Laughing

It is a wonderful sound

That echoes

As if in a tunnel

A pink ribbon is in her hair

And it bounces

As she runs

VI

She stops at a swing set

In the woods

And mounts the swing

With her hands on the chains

High above her head

Perfectly still and still perfectly expressionless

Not swinging

Until a man

Comes up to her

And makes her smile

VII

He is a shadow

At first

As if the dream

Is taunting me

And then he becomes clearer

He walks behind her

And begins to push

Higher and higher

And her laughter with his

Is music

VIII

It is not my father

But I am glad for her

His face and hers

Are filled with happiness

As the swing swings higher

Until he stops it

From moving

And she runs from it and him

Across the lawn

Running faster and faster

19

IX

I watch him
Alone at the swing
Staring after her
Sad
His short dark hair
Thinning
And parted on the left
His beard a shadow
On a handsome
Face

X

And then she is alone again
Standing by a wooden bridge
Her hands on her face
And she is crying
No
Whimpering
And I recognize those sounds
I sit up in my bed
And listen
As they come through my closet door

CHAPTER II

Voices

Part 1

I

Her name is Melinda

I don't know how

I know this

But it came to me

In another dream

Someone was calling her

Melinda

And she was standing over me

Staring

Her eyes looking into mine

II

She was

Expressionless again

Nothing betrayed her thoughts

And then

Slowly

Her lips began to move

Upward

And her smile

Beautiful and haunting

Woke me

III

I sat up

With an urgency

To call your number

I found it on your web site

And memorized it for times like this

But the clock

Said midnight

And I knew I couldn't call

I wished that you would finally answer

My emails

IV

I trust you to know

What I am experiencing

My mother's concerned

I will never get her to believe

That spirits like Melinda live here

They call on people

Like us

For help

It is perfectly natural

For those of us willing to believe

V

Do you hear her

A voice

That calls out from somewhere

Soft moans

Or whining

That reach deep inside of you

Begging

Pleading for you to understand

A soft whisper

That says Melinda

VI

Or maybe

Melinda isn't the one calling to you

Maybe

You hear

A male voice

A father who is calling out

To his son

A desperate plea

For you

To talk to me

VII

Billy Joel sang

"Only the Good Die Young"

I play it often in my room

Have you spoken

To many dead people

Who have died young

Are they still here

To talk about their lives

Will they be okay

Was my father killed because he was good

VIII

When you were young

Did your parents say

Finish everything

On your plate

Or you will

Stay there

Until you do

Does God keep us here

Until we finish

Everything we have started

IX

Do you dream
At night
Do you wake in a cold sweat
Knowing that what you have just heard
Is what you were meant to hear
Do they struggle
To end your pain
Through them
Or end their pain
Through you

X

How old were you
When you first began
To hear the voices
Of the dead
Did you keep it secret
Did anyone laugh
Or tease you
Or stop calling
And start
Saying prayers for you

Part 2

I

The voices began

When I was fourteen

My father is the only one

Who knew I heard them

He told me

Not to be afraid

He said they were

Like lost and lonely angels

And that

His voices began at fourteen too

II

Does everyone hear voices

I asked my father

No he said

You and I were chosen as sort of Earth Angels

We are special

Do you only see them in your dreams?

Yes I said

Do they scare you?

No I answered.

Good, you needn't be be afraid

III

Can Mom hear them

I asked

Your mom is the best mother

In the world

He said

But she doesn't understand

So she's afraid

Of what we hear and dream

What do you say

We make your gift our secret

IV

Who are they I asked

People with a message he said

Some have come for your help

Do you want to help them he asked

Yes I said

Good he answered

Me too

Come to me

 If you have any questions

I will be here for you

V

My father is no longer

Alive as he was in this world

And I know he is not dead

His food is still on his plate

He is not finished with his life here

Or me

Why won't he answer

Where has he been for eighteen months

Why is he not

Communicating

VI

The girl in my closet

Melinda

Did not come here

Until one year from my father's death

Did he send her

Is he talking through her

Can he talk through you

Why is it taking him so long to reach me

Can you interpret dreams

From the Other Side

VII

My father said

There are many people

Who say they hear voices

They write books

And movies

And give lectures

But are not truly connected

Why am I not

Connecting

To you

VIII

Do spirits

Have frequencies

Are they like radio waves

That seek transmitters

How do the undead

Reconnect with the living

How do they

Choose their listeners

And reach

Those of us who want to listen

IX

My dreams
Have been taken over
By Melinda
There are no nights now
When she doesn't come to me
She comes out of her closet
A mass of energy
Floating
Until I am pushed
Into my dreams

X

Some dreams
Are too real
And then
They make no sense
They change so quickly
In them I see Melinda
The man at the swings
Comes back in shadows
Is the sad man my father
And the crying Melinda me

Part 3

I

The police
Said my mother
Had to go to the morgue
To identify the body
And I made her take me
To see if I could reach him
He was on a table
With a sheet over his face
And when they lifted it
We saw him

II

He did not appear
To be asleep
His eyes
Were closed
And his face
Was badly bruised
No frown or anger
Or smile
An expressionless face
Like Melinda's

III

I tried to make him hear me
Quietly
From inside my head
And waited for his answer
But it didn't come
And I screamed silently
Are you okay
But there still was no answer
And I stood there waiting
Until I was led away crying

IV

My mother made them tell her
What had happened
A family
Children and parents
In costumes
Hit him head on
And killed him instantly
He was pronounced dead
At the scene
The only fatality

V

They told us
Where the car had been taken
And gave us two boxes
One had all of his personal belongings
His clothes and wallet and jewelry
The other
Was smaller than a breadbox
Wrapped in colorful paper
With a bow and card
That said Happy Birthday Son

VI

The present
Is still in my closet
With Melinda
It is in one corner
And she
Is in the other
I refuse to open it
Until
He says
I can

VII

I don't know

What religion you are

We are Catholics

When people we love

Die

We take them to be embalmed

And then put them

In their caskets

With the lid open

For people to see

VIII

Friends and relatives came for two days

To see my father's body

Surrounded with beautiful flowers

From everyone

And they stood in line

To get the chance

To kneel and see his face close up

One last time

Before never

Seeing him again

IX

The room was filled with chairs

And I sat in the front row

With my mother

To hug and kiss

And shake hands with

All of the guests

Who came to pay their respects

And between the hugs

I sat and stared at him

Waiting

X

On the morning of his burial

I didn't want to go to his grave site

I had never been

To a cemetery

My father didn't like going there

He told me I wasn't ready for it either

And when his hearse pulled in

Our limousine followed

And I knew

Why I should have listened

CHAPTER III

MY FATHER

AND

FRIENDS

Part 1

I

Their voices began in chaos at the gate

All of them talking at once

A cacophony of frantic questions

From everywhere

Hundreds of voices penetrating my skull

I pressed my hands against my ears

Trying to block them out

But the voices came

From somewhere deep

Inside my head

II

I couldn't bear to hear them

And screamed for them to

Stop

And the driver did

I ran from the car

Back to the gate

With my mother shouting behind me

But she let me run

And I stood outside the cemetery gasping for air

Until the voices were finally silent

III

The procession of cars

Passed with their headlights on and continued

To the side of the little road by the grave site

They all thought they understood

And left me to be alone

I watched from a distance

As they crawled from their cars

And surrounded the flowers piled near his coffin

Hundreds of flowers

That died for him

IV

The people stood in a circle

Staring into the center

Where the coffin sat above his grave

And then another car passed me

And parked by them to unload its passengers

A family of four

From a newspaper clipping

In their funeral clothes

Instead of their

Halloween costumes

V

I don't know

If my mother

Let them stay

I turned and walked

For miles

Angry and cursing

At my father

For leaving me

Saying things

He would have never tolerated

VI

Do you go to cemeteries

Can you hear them

Do they

Call out to you

To help them

Are they in pain

Will they ever be free

Why don't I see

Or hear from him

Why can't he talk to me

VII

The light was on when I returned home
And my mother was sleeping in a chair
I went to my room and stood for a long time
Staring at my closet door
Waiting for him to speak to me
My father's present was sitting in there
Where my mother had placed it
And there were no sounds from the closet
Until my birthday
One year later

VIII

When I reached for the box
I felt her energy
Sliding first across
The back of my hand
And then up my arm
Into my neck and shoulders
A chill ran through me
Ice
Then fire
Then comfort

IX

I have never tried

To touch the box since

Can the things

People touch

Before they die

Carry a piece

Of their souls

Can they carry messages

We are meant

To understand

X

What will our spirits

Look like

When we return

Will we look the way we did

At the time of our death

Will we resemble who we were

Or be floating masses of shapeless energy

Only visible on this side

In dreams and visions

That must be interpreted

Part 2

I

In a couple of months

I will graduate

From high school

And I have already made plans

For community college

My father would not have been happy

But we can't afford a four year school

And my mother needs me here

To take care of the house

And her

II

I haven't said much to you

About my friends

There isn't much to say

I've had very little

Contact with them since my father's passing

They are computer geeks

And treat their

Computers

As if they are

Girlfriends

III

Most of their time

Is spent goggling

Over their electronic lovers

They keep snuggled

Near their beds

And they hurry to get home

So they can excitedly run their fingers

Across them

With little time or thought

For anything else

IV

My mother surprised me

This year

With a birthday party

And invited all three of them

Surprise I said

And ignored them

While I sat playing games

And writing diary poems

On my laptop

Until they left

V

George, Todd, Eric
And I
Have been friends since kindergarten
There is very little
We don't know about each other
But I never told them
About my gift
Until my father died
And they listened
But laughed

VI

You realize
Todd said
That this is part of
Your grieving process
You need to believe that he is still here
You need to embrace it
Until you can get over it
And then let him go
You still have us he said
And laughed

VII

Todd is right

George said

We all loved your father

He was great

But nobody lives forever

You have to think about

Where to go from here

Think about college

And your career

Not ghosts

VIII

With your grades and IQ

You can be anything you want

Focus on that Eric said

And do it for your father

We all know what we want to be

And where we want to go

Pick a school

And career

You can't make money

Being a ghost buster

IX

Growing up
Can be scary
One day can change
Everything and everyone
You ever knew.
I stopped hanging with them
And they laughed at first
Saying I should get over it
And then tried to talk more seriously
When it was too late

X

I spend time
Writing poems in my room
Trying to make sense
Of life and death
The way millions of others have done before me
Brilliant people of all religions and some with none
Great minds
And isn't it amazing that not one of them
Has returned to us
With a definitive answer about the After Life

Part 3

I

I have never had a girlfriend

And I am not gay

George sort of has a girlfriend

That he met on line

Todd is his own girlfriend

And Eric is

Openly gay

They will all most likely meet someone

Away at college

While I am here getting to know me

II

My mother

Is a widow

She doesn't wear black every day

Like old women in mourning

But her mind and heart

Are dressed in black

She has no desire

To marry again

But desperately wants a partner

For me

III

I am sure

You have a daughter

Or a cousin's friend

Who needs a boyfriend

Exactly like me

My mother thinks everyone does

She says prayers for good partners

Every day of the week

But I have enough on my mind

With Melinda

IV

The Junior Prom

Was a couple of months

After my father died

George and Todd

Both went with girls

Their mothers got for them

Eric brought

A boyfriend

And made

All the local papers

V

The Senior Ball

Is coming

George is taking

The girl he took last year

Todd has a steady girlfriend

Eric is still not sure who he's taking

And I'm going with

My mother's friend's cousin

Because I'm tired of

Saying no

VI

My mother is driving us

In the car she bought

With the insurance money

She received

From my father's accident

We still have not fully settled

His claim

My mother said when we do

She will quit work

And I will go to a good college

VII

It has been two months

Since I started

Writing to you

I imagine

That you're not even getting these

Why else would you

Not be answering

And though my father

Hasn't answered me either

I won't stop trying to reach either of you

VIII

If people stopped praying

Every time they didn't get answered

There would be no prayers

I know my father

Is trying to reach me

I feel his presence

And I know the key

Is Melinda

She is still in my closet

Opposite the corner from his present to me

IX

She has become
More daring
She moans and whines less
And appears to me more often
Still hovering
Watching
Floating
Rubbing up against me
Wearing my body
Like an old suit

X

And the dreams
Haven't stopped
She comes to me in them
Every night
With her pink ribbon bouncing
And the handsome man
In the shadows
Constantly around her
Watching her
And me

CHAPTER IV

THE ACCIDENT

Part 1

I

I wasn't able to handle

The details of the crash

Or the family that caused it until recently

Even though I had seen them at the cemetery

I feared my reaction

The parents are younger than mine

The son

Is about twelve

And the daughter

Is about nine

II

I went to the library

And looked up what had happened

In our local paper

There was a picture of my father

Young and smiling

And I wanted to burst into tears

I put the paper down

And took a walk

And when I got back

The paper was still there waiting for me

III

It was a dark and stormy night
In some places
Halloween was canceled
Wind tore through neighborhoods
Blowing down trees and power lines
Rain pelted brave trick-or-treaters
Forcing them to re-treat
And the only ones
Foolish enough to be driving
Were rushing home to their families

IV

The McCannisters were returning
From a canceled party
The rain had graduated
To a downpour
And they were less than a mile
From home
On the highway doing 40
When the children began to argue
And their father turned to quiet them
Entering my father's lane

V

Have you ever seen

Flowers by the roadside

Shrines to those who died there

Can souls get trapped

In the spot where they were killed

Can they be forced to linger

And relive their death

Again and again

If it is true and my father was there

He wasn't answering

VI

When I left the spot

Where he died

I walked toward their house

I had no idea what I would say

If I saw any of them

And when I turned the corner

And stood

By their mail box

It was overstuffed

A For Sale sign was on the lawn

VII

Do people

Take their guilt with them

When they die

Are they forced to relive

Their mistakes

Until they are free from them

Do they live in limbo forever

How long does it take

To Cross Over

Can good people go directly to the Light

VIII

What is death

What does it look like

I asked my father

I don't know he said

I know it has to do with the Light

A very bright light

Have you seen it I asked

I have he said

I've watched troubled souls

Walk off into it

IX

Did you help set them free

Yes he said I believe I did

Am I able to help them too

Is that my gift

I believe it is he said

If you want it to be

Would I be able to help you

If you got trapped

I hope so he said

And smiled

X

Can people

Who save

Tortured souls

Go directly

To the Light

Without stopping

And if they do

Will they lose

Their power

To communicate with the living

Part 2

I

I hope you do not find

My diary poems

Annoying

My mother has trouble reading them

She said they are like

Machine gun fire

Shooting ideas at her

I stopped letting her read them

When I was about

Fourteen

II

My father of course

Loved them

He asked me to teach him

How I do it

I just write them I said

As I think of things

It helps me

To focus

And becomes sort of

Poet-therapy

III

Do you have someone

Or something

To help you

When you need

To talk

Do you have a wife

Or son or daughter

To share

Your secrets

And your spirits

IV

My father

Tried to write

Diary poems

But they were not very good

Except the ones

He wrote

About my mother

And me

I told him he should write about the voices

No he said

V

Are you afraid of

Your gift

Do you ask yourself

Why me

Do you spend

Most of your time alive

Thinking about dying

Do you wonder

When all of the questions will stop

And all of the answers will begin to come

VI

Melinda's dreams

Are sometimes so frightening

I wake up

Unable to breathe

I'm in them

Being warned

And I'm trying to understand her

But I can't

I scream at her to make sense

But she doesn't

VII

The man in the shadows

Is in the dreams too

He is laughing

At first

And when Melinda

Talks to me

And I don't understand her

He stops laughing

And begins whining

And I wake up to the noises in my closet

VIII

I dreamed of her one night

When the man wasn't there

And it was as if

She was someone else

We were alone

And her blue eyes paralyzed me

Pulled me inside out

And when she said LET GO and I did

I began falling

At an incredible speed

IX

I was falling faster
And faster
With each second
The fear building inside of me
Frantically I searched for something to grab
Something to break my fall
And there were hands
Attached to corpses
Hundreds of naked bodies
From photos I had seen

X

I wanted to turn from them
But I needed them
To catch me
To stop me from falling
And I screamed for them
To please help me
But my mother came instead
And asked me if I was having
A bad dream
Yes I said

Part3

I

Where do bodies go

Do they unite with the soul

Years and years later

After they are done rotting

Or do they simply become

Recycled dust

Or old rubbish

Or discarded

Cicada shells

Or maybe abandoned caterpillar cocoons

II

Do souls like Melinda

Get lonely

For the living

Do they spend eternity

Pining for what they've lost

Would the dead

Call to the living

Pleading for them to come

To end their loneliness

And cut short their lives here

III

I am not

Contemplating suicide

I don't think my father

Would want me to go to them early

We both know I can only help them from here

But I don't really know Melinda

What if Melinda

Is not

From my father

 At all

IV

Has Melinda

Lost a father

Does she need someone

To talk to

The way that I need you

Would she take me

Into her power

Through my dreams

And convince me to

Join her

V

My mother's friend's cousin's daughter
Wants to meet me
My mother said she will be
The perfect date
She has a great personality
Which in mother-talk
Usually means
She is probably
The ugliest girl
In her graduating class

VI

I wanted to tell her
That I had changed my mind
I didn't want to go
To the stupid Senior Ball
But she said I should
Get out of the house
I would really like her
She is fun to be with
And has long pretty hair
And piercing eyes

VII

Can souls change bodies
Is reincarnation real
Is life here on earth
The beginning
Or end
Of a cycle of lives
Is my father living again
In some other form
Is there any way
To recognize him

VIII

My father and I
Saw a girl once
Who was not like
Other young girls
She said things
And knew things
My father couldn't understand
He called her
An old soul
Can old souls live in new bodies

IX

Can you see old souls

In new bodies I asked my father

I'm not sure he said

But sometimes I think I can

Sometimes people seem so familiar

I swear I know them

Even when

I know

I have never

Seen them before

X

When dogs

Go around

Smelling each other's butts

Do you think

They are trying to find

Their old souls

 I asked my father

He nearly fell off his chair laughing

And then said

I'm not really sure

CHAPTER V

KATIE

Part I

I

When the doorbell rang

My heart nearly stopped

I knew who was on the doorstep

My mother had invited

Her friend's cousin's daughter

Katie

To dinner

So we could

Get to know each other

Before our first date

II

I felt the sweat beading up

In my arm pits

And my hand

Was actually shaking

When I opened the door

There they were

Mother and daughter

Neither of them

Even coming close

To looking like Melinda

III

I guess I was staring

Because my mother said

Where are your manners

Invite them in

Katie wasn't anything I imagined

I wanted to take a picture of her

And send it to the geeks

They would have crapped their pants

And said I rented her for the photo

Then reality hit

IV

Did you ever realize

That you were too awake

Did you wish you really were dreaming

Because what you had was too good to be real

Why would someone like Katie

Ever want someone

Like me

And then I glimpsed her

In the mirror behind me

And she was shaking her head yes at her mother

V

Melinda has long blonde hair

And piercing blue eyes

Katie

Is a brunette

With warm hazel eyes

That are almost green

Her nose turns up

And her freckles

Look like they were placed there

Do you believe in love at first sight

VI

I couldn't take my eyes off of her

And my mother

Gave me the

Don't-Do-That look

But I did it anyway

And I think Katie

Liked it

Because she was staring back at me

Both her eyes and her freckles

Looked like they were dancing

VII

After dinner

Our mothers let us

Take a walk together

And I can't believe I

Took her hand as we walked

And she let me

I didn't think you would be

So good looking she said

I was so surprised

I squeezed and almost broke her hand

VIII

I told her

I was sorry

And then I said

Squeeze mine

And she said

What

I said I want to be sure I'm not dreaming

And she smiled an amazing smile

And I said

Will you come to the dance with me

IX

When we got back into the house

My mother asked if we enjoyed our walk

It was okay I said

And Katie looked shocked

So I burst out laughing

And she smacked me

She actually smacked me

And we both cracked up laughing

When she left to go home

I wished she didn't

X

I told my mother I really liked Katie

And hurried to my room

Because I knew

Something was not right

It was too perfect

Too unreal

No noise was coming from the closet

So I sat on my bed and waited

For this dream

To suddenly end

Part 2

I

I sat for nearly

One hour

Thinking about Katie

And Melinda

And my father

Did he send her

Is it possible

For the dead to manipulate life

Has he become

My guardian angel

II

I jumped

When I heard the knock at my door

It was my mother

Smiling

And telling me that the phone

Was for me

I don't have a cell phone because I don't like phones

But we talked

For four hours

And then switched to emails

III

We talked about everything

School, neighbors, friendships

And fathers

I told her about mine

And she told me about her parents'

Divorce

Her father lives far away

And she hasn't seen him in over a year

She's an only child

Like me

IV

Did you ever say something

You wish you didn't say

Did you share a secret

You were not supposed to share

And then wait to see if

Something would happen

I wanted to tell her that I have been writing

Diary poems to you

About my father who had a special gift

But I couldn't tell her

V

Katie said

Her father's only gift to her

Was leaving

All her parents did was fight

And hate each other

He still loves Katie

But he is not able to communicate with her

Just yet

It hurts but she sort of understands

Can I teach her how to write diary poems

VI

Katie lives a few miles from us

It's way too far to walk

And she doesn't go to my school

But no place is too far

For telephones or computers

And when I finally got to bed

That first night I met her

It wasn't until three in the morning

The minute I fell asleep

I started dreaming

Melinda

Was at the wooden bridge

Crying

And the man from the shadows

Was standing over her

The man reached out his hand

And Melinda pulled away

The man reached for her again

And she tried to run

But the railing gave way

VIII

I heard myself

Screaming

I wanted to reach for her

To save her

I could see her falling down

Faster and faster

And the corpses' hands were reaching out

To catch her but they couldn't

And my mother's voice

Asked me if I was having another bad dream

IX

I was still awake

When the sun came up

Melinda's whimpering

Would not let me sleep

And she had entered me somehow

I could feel her

Wearing me

Writhing under my skin

Trying to find a place

To be safe

X

It was Saturday

And there was no reason to get out of bed

Except to check my email

So somehow

I fell into a dreamless sleep

I awoke with a start

And ran to the computer

I was hoping there would be an email

From Katie

There were thirty-six

Part 3

I

They started with

I just wanted to say good morning

And ended with something like

If you are not alive

I will never forgive you

I sat there staring at the screen

Not believing

She was real

And then I touched the screen

To help myself see her again

II

I wrote her a diary poem that said

You will be happy to know

(I hope)

That I am still alive

And would love to see you again

If it's okay with you and your mother

We can go for pizza or something later today

To talk about the dance

If you can't or it's too soon to see me again

Maybe we can go another time

III

My mother was thrilled

When I told her about the pizza date

She said she would drive me

And Katie's mother could drive her

We could all have pizza together

Oh yeah what a great idea

I said

No

Don't even

Think about it

IV

It took about an hour

To figure out

What to wear

I finally settled on a red flannel shirt

And jeans

Then I combed my hair

About twelve times

Before I left for the car

I touched my closet door

But didn't hear or feel a thing

V

We got to the pizzeria first

And got a booth

My mother sat with me

And when Katie came in with her mother

We all stood and stared for a minute

She was wearing a red flannel shirt

And jeans

We all laughed hard

And then at almost the exact same time

Said okay good-bye to our mothers

VI

The waitress came over

And I asked if I should order a whole pizza

Yes she said with pepperoni

Do you like pepperoni

I do I said

Good she answered

I'm starving

We didn't say much for a while

And just when she was about to ask me something

They must have come in

VII

Katie

Doesn't look like other girls I know

She doesn't wear make-up

Or have a fancy hair-do

She's sort of a country-girl

And I was so busy admiring her

I didn't see them until they were in front of us

Check this out Eric said

The look on all three of their faces

Was priceless

VIII

They would have stared all day

With their mouths wide open and speechless

And it felt so good I almost let them

But I said

This is Katie

Katie this is George, Todd and Eric

Holy Shit Todd whispered

It's amazing to meet you George said

Okay

You can all go now I told them

IX

Todd, Eric and George
Sat in a booth on the far side gawking
While I sat eating and talking
With Katie
She wanted to know all about them
And I told her how long we had been friends
She asked if they were going to the dance
I said I didn't know because we weren't really
Talking right now
But didn't tell her why

X

We ate the whole pizza
And then we discussed
The dance
I can't believe it's next week
She said
Are you sure you want to take me
You can change your mind if you want
I looked up at her and smiled
And then I saw something strange
In the center of her hazel eyes

CHAPTER VI

THE
CEMETERY

Part 1

I

That night

Melinda spoke to me

She hovered over my bed

And when I

Opened my eyes

Hers were staring

Into mine

You mustn't fear the voices

She said

Go to the cemetery

II

I awoke as I usually do

From dreams like that

Cold and sweaty

My room was totally silent

I looked at my closet and stared

Through the darkness

Then got up from my bed

When I went to open my closet door

It opened

By itself

III

I could barely breathe
I thought for sure my mother
Would be knocking at the door
My heartbeat seemed almost deafening
Slowly I fell to my knees
And as I reached for my father's present
Melinda did as she had done before
She entered me through my hand
And climbed through me slowly
Until every part of me was filled with her

IV

I stayed on my knees for what seemed to be hours
Frozen to the spot
And a dream passed through me
As if each of the thoughts in the dream were mine
Melinda was with the man
From the shadows
But his face was clear
And he was holding Melinda's hand
They were standing by a grave stone
Looking out toward the gate

V

They turned to each other

And the same dream I had before

Began to play again

Melinda

Was at the wooden bridge

Crying

And the man from the shadows

Was standing over her shouting

The man reached out his hand and grabbed her

Melinda pulled taking both of them over the edge

VI

I heard myself

Screaming

I wanted to reach for them

To save them

I could see them falling

Faster and faster

And the corpses' hands were reaching out

To catch them but they couldn't

And my mother's voice

Asked me if I was having another bad dream

VII

Her hand touched my shoulders from behind me

And I jumped when I felt her

I thought she was Melinda

She helped me to my feet

And led me to my bed

Then sat beside me

Do you hear the voices

She asked

Is someone in your closet

Has your father come back

VIII

No

I said

I haven't heard from him yet

I thought you might hear the voices

The way he did

She said

You knew about his voices

I asked

Yes she said

But I never let him talk about them

IX

Were you afraid of them I asked

Terrified she said

I thought if he

Told me about them

They would start visiting me

And I knew I couldn't handle it

Are you still afraid I asked

I am still terrified

But I want you to tell me

Everything

X

We sat until the sun came out

And I didn't miss a detail

I read her every email

I've written to you

When I was done

She said I should sleep for awhile

And then

We should go

Together

To the cemetery

Part 2

I

My mother was sitting at the table

She was fully dressed and ready

And so was I

We got into the car without talking

And drove straight to the cemetery gate

As we approached

I felt myself shaking

I wanted to run from the car

But she was there inside of me

Forcing me to continue on

II

I held my breath

And listened for the deluge

But nothing came

My mother looked at me

As if to say are you okay

I don't hear them I said

I think Melinda asked them not to speak

She doesn't want me to be afraid and is with me

And I'm sure my mother said

That your father is with us too

III

She pulled bravely to the side of the little road

And turned off the engine

Then we went to his stone

I expected to hear his voice then

And begged him to say something

But there was silence

My body began to move without me

I walked as my mother followed

To a stone near my father's grave

And my mother gasped

IV

The stone read

Rest In Peace

Melinda Johnson Age 9

And my skin began to tingle

Burn

And I wanted to run

But my feet were anchored to her grave site

And when my feet were free to move again

They went to the stone

Next to Melinda's

V

I could see his sad face in my mind

As clearly as it had appeared

In my dream

And then I heard the weeping

My mother was crying

I know this story

She said

It happened over 20 years ago

Right after we moved in

It was heart breaking

VI

The whining was deafening

It came from inside of me

And then became a whimper

As my mother told the story

That made the headlines

Of the man who killed his daughter

And himself

Rather than lose

His family

To divorce

VII

She's still alive

I screamed

My mother stared at me in disbelief

Melinda she asked

It can't be

Her mother I said

She's still alive Melinda is communicating with me

My mother put her hands to her mouth

And through her tears she said

I know where she lives

VIII

I bent before my father's grave

And kissed it

Before going to the car

And as the engine started

I heard a slow murmur

It began to rise and get louder

They were starting to talk

All of them at once

And I begged my mother

To hurry out of the cemetery gates

IX

The house was less than two blocks

From ours

Unkempt and sorrowful

My insides were ready to explode

And I wanted desperately to leave there

But I knew I couldn't

I had to take her in there to tell her mother the truth

About Melinda and the accident

My mother rang the bell and an old woman

Stood before us

X

Are you Mrs. Johnson

My mother asked

The whining inside of me

Became a painful whimpering

No the woman said

And my mother and I stood there

Confused and speechless

What do you want of her

The woman asked

She is not well

Part 3

I

My mother lied

And said we were old friends

Making a Sunday visit

The woman was skeptical

But allowed us into the bedroom

Where Melinda's mother lay dying

I began to cry as I saw her frail body

Are you death she asked

I thought you'd be bigger

She said and attempted a smile

II

My son has a special gift my mother said

You needn't tell me why you've come she answered

I have always known it was an accident

And I knew she would find a way to bring me peace

Bring her to me

I walked closer to the bed and it was as if Melinda

Began electrocuting me

The woman took my hand in hers

And Melinda flowed through me with a force that

Drained me of my strength

III

My mother was terrified and sobbed loudly
As the woman's eyes closed
She was smiling motionless and peaceful
And then
Her eyes jerked open
Her voice was weak and barely audible
We have something for you she whispered
She pointed to her night stand
And there exactly as I had remembered it
Was the pink ribbon Melinda had worn in my dream

IV

I let go of the woman's hand
And took the ribbon
May you both
Have peace I said
She took my hand in both of hers
And may your own entry
Into the Light she said
Be as peaceful
As you have made
The possibility of ours

V

We were dismissed

The other woman walked us to the door

My sister knew you would come some day

She said

She waited patiently and painfully

God bless you

For bringing

My niece home to us

Your reward

Will be in a better world

VI

When we got into the car

I felt strange

Empty

But happy

I turned to say something to my mother

Who was crying

I should have been more understanding

She said

I should have shared these moments

With your father

VII

When we got into the house
I went directly to my room
And opened the closet door
Melinda
Was not there of course
I reached into my pocket
And took out the pink ribbon
And placed it in her corner
But before I shut the door
I checked for the box with my father's present to me

VIII

At the computer
There were sixty-three emails from Katie
Four from George, twelve from Eric
And none from Todd
I opened Katie's first
And didn't know where to begin
So I invited her to come over
And two minutes after I pressed "send"
The phone rang
You'd better have a good excuse she said

IX

I went downstairs

To thank my mother

For coming with me

She was sitting in

My father's chair

With his picture in her lap

I miss him so much

She said

I would give anything to see

Those hazel eyes alive again

X

Katie

Is coming over

I said

I want to open

Dad's present

And can't do it alone

I want

To open it

With the three

Of you

CHAPTER VII

Coincidences

Part 1

I

Katie came with her mother

And my mother asked

If we should go to my room

Not yet I said

Is there something wrong

Katie asked

No

I said

I have something

To tell you

II

We sat on my bed

And I started at the beginning

The way I did with my mother

Before I knew it

She was sitting there wide-eyed

And crying

I love what you can do

She said

And I love what you did

for Melinda

III

Are you frightened by my ability to talk with them

Not even a little

She said

I think it's wonderful

That you can speak to them

And I want to read all of your diary poems

Some of them are about you I said

They'd better be good things she answered

There is nothing bad about you

I told her

IV

She leaned into me

And I kissed her on the lips

The tingling started somewhere inside me

I almost thought Melinda had returned

But recognized it as my own heat rising

We kissed again

And my mother interrupted us

Is it time

She asked

For what Katie asked

V

I told her

My father brought a gift

For me the day he died

When I spoke with him the day before

He said it was something special

Is it smaller than a breadbox I asked

Yes he said but much more meaningful

I told her I hadn't opened it yet

Would she like to open it with me

Oh my God yes she said

VI

Katie's mother was still in the room

And I let her stay

I knew my father wouldn't mind

I didn't want to be alone when I opened it

All of their eyes were on me

As I brought the gift to the bed

My hands were shaking

It was heavier than I remembered

I removed the card and untaped the paper slowly

Way too slowly for Katie and our mothers

VII

They were hand-written books

I opened the envelope and read the card

Dear Son

If you are reading this

I am already gone

I would have taken this off the box

If I was wrong about my premonition

I am afraid of what may happen today

But can do nothing

To stop it

VIII

I suspect that my dream

Has become a reality

Your mother and your new friends surround you

But I don't know how much time has passed

I wish I could have been there

But I have been called

To where I was destined to be

I suspect that all I anticipated

About Melinda has already happened

Well done if it has

IX

It is my hope

That she is the first

Of many souls

You will save

But you will not do it alone

If you have not met her yet

You will, she is an Earth Angel too

It is your fate to be with her

Recognize her by the color of my eyes

And by the gift she will develop

X

I looked up at Katie

And she was smiling

It started when I was fourteen

She said

But I've kept it secret

I stared at her in disbelief

And then continued to read his letter

Note that I have written this in diary poems

Thank you for teaching me how to write them

You will find more in the books I've written for you

Part 2

I

His diary poems

Were the most amazing things

I have ever seen

They are his thoughts

And experiences of

All the souls he has encountered

Through his lifetime

They are his questions

And his answers

About the After Life

II

I know now

Why I couldn't reach him

His many years of soul saving

Earned him his immediate

Right of passage

To the Light

Beyond the troubled souls and the ability to

Communicate

A right that Katie and I

Hope to earn someday

III

He said he would love

To take credit for Katie

But she was always meant

To be with me

We are destined for greatness

His poems would guide us

Into sharing and understanding the purpose of life

On earth and in limbo

A time for living and loving

For repenting and dying and eternal peace

IV

There are no

Insignificant people

And no such thing

As coincidence

All that happened to me

And *will* happen to me

Is in the books

And has always been

We must accept who we are

And who we must be

V

The night we opened the gift
We received two phone calls
Mrs. Johnson
Died peacefully
In her sleep
There would be no wake or open casket
Or visiting hours
She was content to have lived a full life
And grateful
To be reunited with her loved ones

VI

The second call was from Katie
Am I upset that I am destined
To be with her
Yes I said
Just kidding
Not funny she said
And guess what
She got a call from her father
Who is sending her a ticket to come visit him
She's going for a week sometime after the dance

VII

I don't know if you will ever read these

But my writing them

Has brought focus

And importance to my life

I said when I began

Writing to you

That I believed dead people live here

I know now they do

I said I was helpless without you

I'm not

VIII

Perhaps someday

Our paths will cross

And I can thank you

For what you have helped me to do

In the meantime

I have a tux to rent

And a limo to share

With George

Eric

And Todd

IX

By the way
I had a dream
The night we opened my father's gift
Melinda's father was at the bridge
And Melinda came to him and smiled
They turned together holding hands
Standing at their stone in the cemetery
They were looking at the gate waiting for someone
And then her mother
Came to join them

X

There was another person in the dream
A man in the shadows
I couldn't see his face
But when he turned
To walk into the woods
Melinda and her parents followed him
And a beautiful bright light appeared
After they walked into it
They turned to face me
And I saw my father smiling behind them

www.ingramcontent.com/pod-product-compliance
Lightning Source LLC
Chambersburg PA
CBHW020617130626
46552CB00003B/1006